Things

    I

        Should

           Have

              Said

-A compilation of thoughts and emotions-

By Simone

Thing I Should Have Said

Copyright © 2008 by Simone

ISBN- 978-0-6151-8719-8

This book is dedicated to all those who inspired a

letter.

Thank you

Mom, you truly are wonderful.

Isaiah, you enable my heart to beat.

Christopher thanks for pushing.

Dear Reader,

This is not your everyday novel. This is not a love story and it isn't a drama. It is merely a compilation of unfinished business. I did not compile this for your entertainment but rather for your information and inspiration. The letters you are about to read are letters containing thoughts and feelings...thoughts and feelings that should have been expressed before now. It has taken a long time for these emotions to be brought to light and I want to apologize in advance to anyone who may get offended by a letter addressed to them. I have decided not to use real names, but I am quite sure you will know if a letter is to you once you begin to read it.

I hope and pray that this collection of thoughts, feelings and emotions will bring peace, understanding and even closure to all those with

whom things have been unsaid or undone. Please
keep an open mind and an open heart as you
venture into the depths of another persons heart and
mind.

   Thank you for choosing this book today and
if nothing else, I hope these words inspire you to
never leave things unfinished.

Dear Mary Beth,

You remember the time we went out with those guys from Ridgefield? You probably don't, but I remember it quite vividly…

Well, first of all I told my mother that you, me and one of your friends were going to go to the movies and then I would spend the night at your house. She believed me and allowed me to go. We met the guys at Jo-Jo's house; which ironically was the guy I was dealing with. Apparently he was kind of like the leader of the pack, so to speak. He was a good looking guy, funny and had a magnetic air about him. Well anyway, the night started out fine. We went to some hole-in-the wall club that neither of us thought was going to be any good, but it turned out to be exciting. Jo-Jo and I spent a lot of the night bumping and grinding on the dance floor, we were feeling each other's vibe and I was definitely feeling him. Towards closing hours he and I got a little steamy and ended up making out in a corner. When we all met up outside, no one was ready to go home so one of his friends mentioned an after party spot that didn't close until 6a.m. We all decided that's where we wanted to be so we headed over. The basement party was definitely jumping, even more so than the club we had just come from. Again, me and Jo-Jo had some serious vibes going on between us. Now maybe these vibes would not have been so strong if he hadn't been high and I hadn't been tipsy, but nevertheless they were there.

Anyway, after the basement party Jo-Jo invites us back to his house to kick it and since we're all still in party mode so we head on over. When we get there the first thing Jo-Jo brings out is a bottle of liquor, knowing I'm already feeling really buzzed I say no, but you all insist and insist so I partake. I end up drinking so much that I can barely hold myself up. After drinking all this liquor, I had to use the bathroom. Jo-Jo tells me its upstairs so I begin to crawl up the stairs, you thought that was funny...I didn't. When I got out of the bathroom, Jo-Jo was waiting in the hallway. He gestures towards his bedroom and automatically I know what he's suggesting, but I know even in my drunken state that I don't want to have sex with him, so I begin to crawl back down the stairs. About halfway down, he starts to drag me back up and you're downstairs laughing your ass off all the while I'm saying, "No, I don't feel like it. I don't want to go upstairs. I want to go back down." I admit, that my resistance might not have been strong or outrageously loud, but I know I resisted. I remember him bringing me into his room and putting me on his bed. He pulled up my skirt and did what he had intended to do all night. I *remember telling him that I just wanted to go back downstairs. I remember trying to push him away and in my mind I was fighting as hard as I could, but my body just would not cooperate. It was like I suddenly had bricks attached to my limbs, I couldn't hold them up. When he was done and we were both back downstairs, I remember one of his friends pointing to his shirt, letting him know that my blood was all over it.*

You were supposed to be my friend. You let that guy get me drunk out of my mind, while you laughed. You bitch! You were supposed to look out for me but instead you let me get raped. I'll never forget that night and I'll never forgive you for letting that happen to me.

Dear B. Land,

Well, I am not quite sure what to say to you and if I should even be speaking to you. I heard from a mutual friend of ours that you work with my boyfriend. Is that true? I know I told you that he and I were having issues, but I truly do love him. I was honest when I said I was attracted to you, but I was also being very, very honest when I told you that I love him and don't want to do anything to jeopardize his love for me. Maybe it is too late for that, maybe I have already crossed the line, though nothing physical has occurred between us. I feel guilty for even speaking to you now. This is not a good feeling. I would hate to loose him over a flirty conversation I have with you.

I don't want to lead you on and I will always remain honest with him, you and myself. I do find you attractive and I think what heightens my attraction to you is that he and I are at odds with one another. I don't want to get into too much detail about my personal issues with my current boyfriend, but I will say that you are a great listener and I appreciate the attention you showed.

Well, I guess I just needed to clarify things with you. I need you to know that it is not such a good idea for us to be friends. I just don't see that working out very well, with us being attracted to each other. I hope that there are no hard feelings between us and that you find exactly what you're looking for.

Dear Ike C. Steven,

There was no getting away from you. Thank God you never ended up being my boss. I remember days you would come into my office either pretending you were there on business or like you were passing through to see someone else.

I remember one time in particular you came by. You were talking to me and another female from the office. It was just casual conversation about something so random I don't even remember what it was. Well, anyway when you walked away she said to me, 'he thinks you're attractive and if you guys weren't both involved with other people, he would definitely try to get with you'. I was blown away by that because I didn't think we were flirting with each other nor did I feel like we were giving off any signals, but she made it clear that she felt the attraction. I had to cover it up by seeming very uninterested. Hopefully it was believable.

Well, I must say that smile of yours is a killer. After a while I thought you were smiling at me just to get my defenses down and that you were doing it on purpose. You were a cool guy. I liked talking to you and even though I knew you were probably just trying to get in my pants, we did have nice conversations about life in general. I wasn't surprised you were from a poor, urban background, but I was surprised at the kinds of things you were able to talk about. Thanks for not coming at me with 'give me the booty' lines.

I saw you the other day at the store…I had to avoid you because I didn't know what to say or how I would feel. I am still involved and I don't want any drama. I miss that smile though and the nice things you would say to me. I want you to know that our conversations lifted my spirits in a way you may never know. Hope you're doing okay.

Dear L.M. James,

*Our relationship was really screwed up!
After we broke up, you got with some really young
girl, I think barely 18. That threw me off because
you were 23 and I didn't think that was your style.
I know you told me you were hurt, so maybe it was
a silly rebound relationship.*

I think you really loved me though…

*I miss you sometimes…usually when my
boyfriend is being an asshole. I used to think you
were mean until he started showing his true colors.*

*I know you're back in school, I'm proud of
you.*

*Anyway, I think about you from time to
time. Wonder what could have been, but I feel we
would have split anyway. I saw a recent picture of*

you…you still look good. Cut off all that long hair I love though, but it's all good.

Well, I don't have much to say, just wanted you to know I remember you.

Dear Father,

Where do I even begin? There are so many questions that I used want to the answer to. Why don't you want me? Why don't you love me? What did I do wrong? I can't count the number of nights I've cried over not knowing you. Over wondering if you're thinking of me, wondering if you're missing me, wondering if you remember me.

I remember one time I saw you...I was around 8 or 9 and you promised you would call me for my birthday. I sat around waiting all day, hoping that it was you every time I heard the phone ring. I remember asking myself if I was just a bad daughter; not smart enough, not pretty enough, just not enough.

I remember days at school when other students would brag about going to work with their fathers for "Bring Your Daughter to Work Day". I always used to hide the tears until I got home, then I would cry and cry knowing I had no father to go to work with. My mother tried her best to be both mommy and daddy, but there's that special bond, that special something between a father and daughter that she just couldn't provide.

I remember hearing that you had other children, a pair of twins who were supposedly older than I, and I wondered…does he love them more than me? Does he spend time with them? Does he play with them? Does he teach them things? Why won't he love me? Am I not worthy of his love?

You know, you had a lot to do with my searching for acceptance from guys. Searching and longing for a love only a father could give. Not knowing that giving my heart, mind or body to some guy would never fill the void I felt in my soul. You still affect me today. Although I have many,

many things to be thankful for and I have been blessed with other people who love me, there is still an emptiness that I know will never be quite filled. I have a wonderful stepfather who loves me like his own and I am so very grateful to have him in my life, but for me it always comes down to one question. If a man, a stranger not of my own flesh and blood could love me the way he does, how is it that the man from whose loins I came cannot find it in himself to love the very same way.

Dear Keem W.,

Well, we've been corresponding with each other for a little while now and you have been a big help. You helped when I was dealing with self confidence issues and relationship issues. I really appreciate you not coming at me real crazy either. I'm glad you respect my situation.

Sometimes I need someone to talk to and since I can't talk to who I'm with you were so helpful. Man, I know we've never actually met in person, yet I feel like we've been cool for a long time. I don't know if you feel that way too. How do you feel about me? How do you look at me? These are some questions I'm curious to know the answer to.

You're a mature guy (or should I say man), which you should be, you're 35 years old with two kids and an ex-wife so I can only expect maturity from you.

Anyway, I just want to say thanks for being an open ear, you don't even know how much it meant and still means to me. I hope that you find the unconditional love and affection you're longing for. No matter what I do or where I go I will always remember your motivating words.

Dear Daddy,

I know that things haven't always been smooth between us and I know there were times I purposely gave you a hard time. I want to apologize for that. I was a young child going through the emotional ups and downs of puberty and along with that, I was confused about why my biological father didn't want to have anything to do with me. My mother married a good man when she married you.

You didn't have to accept me into your life as your own, but you did. You loved me like I was your flesh and blood. When people would ask how many children you had, you always included me. I never once heard you call me your stepdaughter, at least not when I was around. Thank you for that. I know you love my mother and brothers very much, but it feels good to know you love me just as much.

Dear L. Wood,

How have things been with you, I hope well. I think about you from time to time and although we had some rocky moments in our relationship, I can honestly say I felt good when I was with you. You were always honest about your feelings and thoughts and I thank you for that. It was so easy to be around you, so easy to open up to you. I remember days when you would come to my house after you got off from work and we would sit on my front steps and talk into the wee hours of the next morning. What did we talk about? How come we could talk for so many hours yet I can't remember what we spoke about? I loved the way you held my hand in yours, I love the way you would put your arm around my shoulder to comfort me.

We did have fun, but there was a lot of sadness that surrounded our relationship at times. Let me let you in on a little secret…I was pregnant twice; so I was informed by a doctor at a free clinic. The first time was insane. My mother used to always ask me when was the last time I got my period, which bothered the hell out of me because at the time I was happy when ever it didn't show up. On one occasion, I remember telling her that I wanted to go see a doctor because my period was acting 'weird'. I was bleeding very heavily and I had tremendous pain…then I stopped, thought about it and told her I no longer needed to see a doctor.

One day at school I had a friend of mine take me to the clinic during our lunch hour. He asked what was going on, but I didn't tell him. After the examination was complete, the doctor told me that it looked like I was experiencing a miscarriage and that I should rest, but how was I going to do that? I was not going to tell my mother, she would kill me. I didn't tell you because I was scared.

The second time I got pregnant I decide that I was going to inform you that my period was late. You tripped on me like I was trying to trap you. In my mind, I'm like "Nigga please, ain't nobody trying to have your fucking baby. I've got shit to do. I'm still in high school; I want to go to my prom. I want to graduate in the next two months. You're full of shit if you think I'm trying to trap you. Don't you know I just got accepted to a college I always dreamed of going to. Being pregnant was definitely not in my plans either, so fuck you!" But that isn't what I said to you…I just let it ride because I can just imagine where you were coming from…getting ready to go to college and some chick

tells you she might be pregnant, that messes up
your whole plan, doesn't it? I understand.

Anyway, the pregnancy test I took while
you were standing outside the bathroom door read
negative…but I was pregnant. I knew you would
loose it and think I got pregnant on purpose or
something, I wasn't ready for a baby and I knew my
mom would be disappointed in me, so I got an
abortion. I just let you think I was never pregnant
to begin with…and left it at that. That was so hard
to do. I think I've gotten over it, but at that time it
was the hardest thing I had ever had to do.

Well, enough of that. I hope you're doing
well. I hope you graduated and you now have a
successful career. Best of luck.

Dear Elder,

You sick bastard! I can't believe you tried to act as if what you tried to do was no big deal! Let me tell you how I remember the night in question.

It was a Saturday night and the youth group along with a few other members of the church went on a trip to the city, I think to see a play or something. Nothing about our time there really seemed awkward except an instance where the big group of us had to cross a busy intersection and you held my hand. I was thinking to myself, "I'm sixteen years old; I think I can cross a damn street by myself. What's up with this guy?" But other than that everything else was okay until it was time to go home.

Well, everyone went back to the church where the cars were parked and sorted out who would ride in what car. It so happened that me and some other teens ended up riding with you. You made up the excuse that you had to stop by your job, which was down the street from my house just so you could drop me off last. You nasty prick.

On the ride down that quiet street, you said something only you thought was funny, did a hearty laugh and somehow your hand ended up on my thigh. You thought you were slick, I saw you look at me checking to see what I was going to do. I crossed my leg towards to door so that your hand wouldn't be able to reach my thigh.

I guess you had to follow through with your lie or maybe you thought your workplace would have been a convenient place to do what your perverted mind had concocted. The gate was locked so you had to get out and unlock it; I thought about getting out and running, but where would I go. You were driving; you could have easily just tracked me down in your van. I decided to wait and see what would happen next. We pulled in and parked, you got out a relocked the gate. I thought for sure I was going to regret not running when I had the chance. You walked me into an office area, and told me to have a seat while you picked up the paperwork you said you needed to get. You walked out of the room and pretended to busy yourself. I was busy trying to figure a way out, looking around the room trying to see what I could use as a weapon if the need arose. You came back into the room and I didn't see any paperwork in your hand...I started to worry more. You were talking but I couldn't make out the words you were saying. You got really close to where I was sitting, and leaned over me. My palms were sweating, my knees were shaking and then you made your move. You leaned in for a kiss and I turned my head away. I saw the disappointment in your eyes and I thought it was

over for me. I told you I wanted to go home but I
was scared to get back in the car. As you drove, I
got a close to the door as I could without falling out.
I spoke no words and never looked in your direction.

When you dropped me off, you said you hope
I had fun that night and if not you were sorry. You
fucking apologized! That means you knew what you
were attempting was wrong. You're nasty and I
hope that it was just a one time thing. If you were
or if you still are a pedophiliac I hope you get help. I
fear for your children.

I want you to know that I have gotten to the
point where I have forgiven you, but an apology for
the humiliation you caused me would be nice.

Dear D. Field,

So our marriage is over...well, it seems to have been over before it started. So many things have happened between us. So much hurt and pain between us. Where do I even begin? How do I begin to formulate where we went wrong? Whose fault was it?

We started out cool, just having fun and enjoying each others' company. Then one day our lives took a turn that it could never recover from. I need you to know that I loved you and I still do. I need you to know that I was willing to do anything for you, if you would only ask. I wanted to be your queen and you to be my king. I wanted the story book fairytale that every girl wants. I was there for you, but you never came to me. You went to others with your hurt and pain. You turned to others for the comfort you should have been seeking from me. I wanted to be the shoulder you cried on, but you didn't want to let me see you be weak. You showed others your weakness and showed me your wrath.

I still don't understand what I did wrong, but I guess it's too late now. No one can turn back the hands of time, but so many of us wish we could. So many things I would change between us, so we could be happy together. I miss you and I hope you miss me too.

If we never get back together I hope that you find someone to do the things for you that I couldn't seem to do. I hope you find someone who will treat you the way you deserve to be treated. I hope you find someone who brings out the best in you, because I was clearly unable to do that.

I hope that through all the pain and all the anger that there was some love and some joy shared between us at some point. I know there was...

Dear J. Spelling,

My friends are telling me that you're no good for me. They think you are too possessive and a little bit crazy. What am I supposed to do? I am so caught up in you that I don't know and can't find a way out. They say that you're probably cheating and maybe you are but I can't prove that so I'll just leave it alone.

We argue every morning and make up every day by dinner time. This cycle is getting the best of me but I just can't seem to let go. If you were in my shoes, what would you do? My mind is filled with thoughts of you, my heart is overwhelmed with future plans and my body has been overcome with longing.

I can't seem to shake you. You have gotten under my skin and it itches…it itches so bad. I

Things I Should Have Said

scratch and scratch, but I'm never satisfied. I can't

get rid of you. My friends have even gone to the

extreme of trying to hook me up with other men, but

the only one I want is you.

Something must be wrong with me, because

in my heart or maybe somewhere in my soul I know

you aren't good for me, but you are like a drug. You

are as serious as heroin. You have filled my veins

with yourself, you refuse to leave and I have

developed a dependency. It's like knowing you're

strung out and wanting help, but refusing to go.

I say that I love you and you do the same,

but this can't be love yet it is more than just lust

and infatuation. What will be come of us in the

end? What exactly is the end? I don't think I'll ever

be able to shake you…but I know that if I stay I will

be consumed by you.

You know we aren't good for each other,

you've agreed so why won't you let me go. I won't

*stop calling so you have to stop calling me. I'll
never tell you not to stop by, so just stop asking.
You know we can't keep doing this, so why not
break it off? You keep saying you're tired of things,
so why not just walk away?*

       *Damn, I am in love with the thought
of being in love with you. That must be it, because
love isn't supposed to be like this.*

Dear Annie V.,

You were a good friend to me. I remember the only thing we really had in common was our age and that we lived in the same city. You were my next door neighbor and you were my best friend. There were no obligations between us. You didn't need anything from me and I didn't need anything from you. We just were just two little 7 year old girls who wanted to play.

I went to a public school which coincidentally was across the street from our houses. You went to a private school that was across town. There were days when I got home early and would sit by my kitchen window waiting for you to get home. By the time you got home, I usually had my homework done already, so I would have to wait for you to finish yours. When we finally got a chance to play, we didn't have very long but we played till it got dark and our mother's had to call us in. There were times we would tell our mothers we weren't hungry, just so we could play longer. Then there were the weekends…the weekends, neither one of us saw the inside of our house unless we had to use the bathroom. We played from the time we woke up to the time our mothers made us come in.

I hated having to leave. The day my mother told me we would be moving, I cried. I thought about all the fun times we had shared together. I thought about how you didn't judge me for being different. I couldn't imagine making another friend like you anywhere she was thinking about moving me to. I was devastated. I wondered how she could do this to me. How could she take me away from this place? I loved my family and the friends I had made. How would I possibly be able to deal with a new neighborhood, how would I make new friends?

I thought we were going to keep in touch. We promised each other we would, but we didn't. I missed you so much when I got to the new city. I wished so much I could move back and I tried to visit every possible chance I got. I resented my mother for a very long time for moving me away from my dear friend.

I guess I just want you to know that I remember you and I hope that things have gone well for you. I hope that you are successful and happy.

Dear God,

What have I done to deserve this sorrowful life you have given me? Why so many sleepless nights and tear-filled days? Who have I wronged and how can I make it right? I know and believe that you exist, but sometimes I wonder if you have enough love and mercy left for me. I feel so unaccomplished so unachieved…so worthless. I see others around me, my peers doing so much with their lives and living their dreams and I think to myself, 'I will never reach my goals, my dreams will never come true'.

I know that I am a sinner and that I am unworthy of your grace, but there are times when I see others gaining so much and I wonder why I can't be happy. I feel like I have been begging, pleading and asking all my life… 'Why can't I be happy? I just want to be happy'. There are times

Things I Should Have Said

when I say to myself, who am I to judge? I am no better than these people, but I am no worse either so why is it that they prosper and I don't.

Maybe I am just asking too much. Maybe I don't deserve the things I ask for or maybe, just maybe I wouldn't know how to handle it if my requests were granted. Is that the reason I am not allowed happiness? Is that the reason every little ounce of joy I receive is quickly taken away?

There have been times when I've wanted my life to be over. So many times I've wished to fall asleep and never wake up. So many times I have put myself in harms way so my life could end. For so many years I have been living in sorrow and pain. Painful memories of tragedies. Truth be told, if it weren't for my beautiful baby ...I don't know what would become of me.

Dear Mom,

I just want to say thank you for always being there for me. I want you to know that although I may not have said it or showed it before, that I appreciate all the things you have done for me. You kept me fed, clothed and there was always a roof over my head. You taught me right from wrong and the importance of an education.

You are a strong woman who has endured many trials and I wish there was more I could do for you to show you how much I love you. I wish I could take away all of your sadness, I wish I could make it so that you were always worry free. I am a part of you and you are a part of me and no matter where I go or who I become I know that your love for me is unconditional and that I can always come home.

You are an amazing woman and you deserve every bit of happiness the Lord blesses you with. You have a big heart and a giving soul which makes people gravitate toward you. You are honest and kind. You are giving, yet firm. I know that one day you will be in heaven, because you are truly an angel here on earth. Never, ever change.

Dear D. Field,

Today marked the day that we exchanged vows to one another…exactly two years to the day. Wow, two years and how it sometimes seems to have been an eternity, and at others only a few months.

Today I spent most of my time alone and you spent most of the day around the house. We did no celebrating for there is nothing to celebrate. I wonder if it occurred to you at some point through out your day that today was our two year anniversary. It sure did occur to me….more than once. Did you wish we were having a joyous and romantic day together? I did. I wondered if things were better between us would we be enjoying each other the way we are supposed to.

Things I Should Have Said   43

I noticed that neither of us mentioned it…almost avoiding it. Did you avoid it on purpose? I think I did subconsciously, although there were no moments between us that would have triggered it. I thought about how nice it would have been if we had a romantic candle lit dinner and spilled our emotions and thoughts to each other while staring into each others eyes, but silly me. I've got to stop day dreaming, right? Right!

This is all so much more than I had anticipated. I thought everything would be ok. I thought that we would be able to work it out no matter what, but I see now that I was wrong. Changes have to be made and I don't see you making any moves toward that. I feel so alone…

I am married (technically) and I have a beautiful and healthy baby. I have what most would consider a family…yet I feel so, so alone. I can't talk to you; you refuse to talk to me. I'm cautious about asking you questions and you just don't even

bother. Why is this happening? Where did we make

a wrong turn? Can we ever make it right again?

Dear K.V.,

I think you should know that I was aware all along that you and Houston had a thing going on. Everyone knew you were head over heels in love with this guy…well at least I knew. It was plain as day and the way you went about denying it made it even more obvious. The more you tried to hide it, the more it showed.

Yes, he and I had a little minor relationship when we were young. We were babies…thirteen and fourteen. How serious could we have been if it only lasted a summer? So what he and I dated, it still showed you were sprung over him, maybe not while I was with him but definitely later on. Come to think of it, your feelings for him are why you would trip over every little thing.

Now, I want to let you know that I did not appreciate you keeping it a secret from me. If we were supposed to be best friends, you should have come to me from the beginning with it and how dare you wait till years later to tell me, with the excuse that you thought I would get upset about it. Your ass waited till I was married and had a child before telling me. I don't know what you call it, but that shit is foul. I mean, I don't have any feelings for him in that way and I haven't since that summer I was thirteen but damn, what if I did?

I respect the fact that when I went to him and asked him if you two had a thing going on, he was truthful. He had no reason to lie. He and I both knew that our relationship was strictly platonic…we knew that we were nothing more than friends and there was nothing to hide. You on the other hand lied and pretended that I couldn't see that you two had something going on. You acted like he was just a good friend. Please!

It's because of your secretiveness why you two didn't work out. You acted like you were ashamed of him. I can understand why he felt the way he did. He liked you and I think he liked you a lot, but maybe due to his situation, he wasn't quite ready for what you were trying to put on him. Maybe he wasn't ready to be in a seriously committed relationship. And on top of that, you have to have things your way or it's the highway and guess what honey…no relationship works like that. If you loved and cared about him the way you acted…or should I say, tried to hide, you would know that it takes compromise to make a relationship work. You couldn't have expected to treat him the way you did and believe he would stick around.

Now, I'm not saying I know everything about what went on between you two, but the little…very little that I gathered from both of you, it wouldn't have worked out any way. You shouldn't

have kept that a secret from me. It makes me

wonder…what else you have kept from me. Have

there been other secret relationships?

Damn it, it's just the principle of it all…

Dear J. Spelling,

Damn, I gotta say you were the type of guy that had me head sprung from the door. I don't know if it was because you were older than I was, but I had dated guys your age before. I mean, you only had three years on me, so I don't think that was it.

You had this swagger that was so damn sexy. I wouldn't call you conceited but you had this attitude about you that said...'I'm the man in charge, I'm runnin' this'. And damn did that shit turned me on.

Let me back track for a second...I'm sure you remember how we met and how I lied to you about being older than I was. I just thought you were so cool that I had to say what I could to keep you interested. I mean our first conversation was all that. I was feeling you and you were feeling me, then it got to that age question. You were 19 and so I decided to tell you I was 17, so you would stay interested, especially because I remember you saying that you weren't trying to deal with no young chicks. So I lied. You were digging me and I was digging you and that's all either one of us needed to continue on with our correspondences.

Do you remember how I paged you one day and told you that I had lied to you? If I remember correctly, I was on the verge of tears because I was so afraid you wouldn't want to deal with me anymore. But you didn't trip. You knew the truth and I told you to do with it as you pleased. You respected my honesty and maturity and told me it didn't matter, you were already feeling me too much to just let it go, but you were glad that I came to you in the beginning rather than wait till we were in too deep. Damn, was I happy to hear that.

Now even though we got past the age situation, we seemed to argue every time we spoke…or at least once a day. I mean, I would page you, you would call back and we'd talk for a while…but sooner or later there was something to argue about and what's crazy is that up to this point we hadn't even see each other in person. Our feelings and emotions and passions were driven solely off of a mental attraction. It would be the same thing every day. You were sick of arguing and I was sick of patching things up, yet neither one of us wanted to be the first to call it quits. We didn't want to call it quits…that was never even brought up in conversation, believe it or not.

I remember the day came where you finally had the time off from work to come see me. I couldn't believe you were going to come all the way from Long Island to see me. I was so nervous, my palms were sweating and I paced back and forth on my front steps waiting to see you walk down the street.

When I first saw your face I knew it was you. Not because you told me what you would be wearing, because you didn't. Not because you had any signs of who you were, but just by the way you walked. I was like damn…that's my man. You looked nervous, but confident and sexy at the same time.

Man, I'll never forget that day. Your eyes were almond shaped and your lashes were long and thick. I could tell that by your complexion you had mixed heritage. I could see the Puerto Rican and I could see the Trinidadian you had described to me over the phone. You were so sexy to me and I could tell by the way your eyes lit up that you were feeling me too.

When you left later on that day, I just knew you would never call me again or so I thought. You told me to page you two hours after you left, just to give you time to get back and I so obediently did. You called me back right away as always and it felt good to know that our mental connection wouldn't be torn down by lack of a physical one.

I don't really remember the details of how we fell apart but I want you to know that I still think of you from time to time and hope you are doing well. I think that my relationship with you is part of the reason why I am so confrontational in my relationships now.

Dear D. Field,

I don't know what has happened but I do know how I feel and I don't like the way I feel. You have so much pride...so much so that you are willing to loose me and jeopardize your relationship with your child. It's got to be your pride. I know that people don't like to be backed up into a corner by an ultimatum, I know but there was no other way for us to get over this bridge without it. The choice you made wasn't me and our family and I am hurt by that. I'm distraught that the other option even appealed to you. What do I lack? What is missing? Because of the choice you made, I'm now picking myself apart trying to find the specific flaw that made it hard for you to choose me.

I love you so much... I wanted to make you happy. I wanted to treat you like a king, but now that's all gone. My daydreaming has caused me a broken heart. I knew this would happen, I didn't want to believe it, but that's just how it goes in my world. Happiness is always temporary.

I sit around and ask myself what's wrong with me? Why don't you love me? What can I do to make you love me and care about me? What can I do to appeal to you? What am I doing wrong? What is she doing right? Why she is so important or better yet, why is she more important than I am? Why don't you care about the pain you cause my heart? Why do I let you make me feel so small? Why do I let you take away my self confidence?

I know it seems as if all I've been doing for the past week or so is cry, but that's the only way I know how to get over someone. I just cry, until I've cried them away. I know that crying won't change the decision you have made and I know that there is nothing left for me to do but accept it and move on…but it's so hard. I had so many plans for us, for our family. What do I tell my mother who prays for our prosperity every day? What do I tell our child?

I know I haven't always been the easiest person to deal with…I know. I know there have been times when I hurt you and I am truly sorry for any pain I've caused you. The tears I've shed over past loves pales in comparison to the amount of tears I've shed over you. This isn't how it is supposed to be.

…I can't see through the tears that currently flow down my face, so I must say goodbye…

Dear M. Tiller,

When I moved away, I felt like I was loosing the sister I never had. We were related, but I felt so much closer to you than just a cousin. I was three years younger than you were but you never treated me like a little kid. You made me feel like I was cool enough to hang out with your group of friends and you allowed me to.

I know that we are both grown now and we have our own families to deal with but I wish we could mend the friendship that was destroyed only by distance. I just know that if we had had the chance to grow up together we would be inseparable now. Our children would play together and be just as close as we once were.

I used to be so jealous of you. I thought you were so pretty and you had the voice of an angel. I still wish sometimes that I could sing like you. I hope you haven't given up on that, you had talent.

I hope that where ever you are and what ever you are doing that you always remember and the good times we had. I hope that you are doing well and that you are happy and successful. I pray that one day our paths will cross again and we can rebuild the sisterhood we once had.

Kiss the baby for me.

Dear God,

I know I complain, but I have so much to be thankful for and I want to thank you right now.

I would like to thank you for the wonderful parents you have blessed me with. It feels good to know that I have a mother that I can call any time to talk about anything. It feels good to know that if I needed to, her doors are always open and I can always go home. I want to thank you for the father you brought into my life when my own refused to live up to his responsibilities. It feels good to know that he loves me and will always be there to protect me and do his best to see that I am happy.

I want to thank you for the trials and tribulations that I have had to endure, because without them I wouldn't be the individual I am today. I know I sometimes ask you why me? But why not me? I have gone through much in my short years, and my pain is no one else's but my own, but so many other people have gone through much worse and have made it through.

I want to thank you for my beautiful baby boy that you blessed me with after doctors told me I would have a hard time conceiving and carrying a child. He is healthy, strong and intelligent and I want to give thanks for him. I pray that you bless me with the knowledge and wisdom to raise him the way you would want me to.

I want to say thank you for the little things that so many of us take for granted and barely appreciate. I want to say thanks for the air that I breathe and the food that I eat. So many people are suffering in other countries from starvation and malnutrition. I have to say thank you for the roof over my head and the ability to provide not only the bare necessities for my son, but for so much more,

Thank you.

Dear Son,

They said I would have a hard time getting pregnant and that even if I did, I probably wouldn't be able to carry the child to full term... meaning, I would have a miscarriage. They told me not to get my hopes up, yet they told me to be positive. I started to believe the negativity and gave up hope. I had finally come to realize that I would never have the privilege of experiencing what almost every woman dreams.

The truth is that your father and I were just two young kids fooling around and enjoying each others company a bit more than we had anticipated. When the doctor told me I was pregnant, I didn't know how to feel. I was glad I now knew that I could conceive but scared at what your father would say or do. I didn't know how to tell him or rather if I should tell him. I didn't know how he would take it.

I thought about getting an abortion because I wasn't ready to be a mother and more so I was petrified. I know your father was scared too, he had to be but he played it cool. I know and I'm sure many others know that you weren't planned, but now that I have you in my life...I would go insane if anything ever happened to you. What would become of me if I didn't have you to keep me grounded, motivated and inspired?

I know that I may not be the best mother but the love I have for you is unconditional, unlimited and incomparable to any other. When you are old enough to read this I pray that you know I tried my best to provide for you and make you happy. You are only a baby right now but I want you to one day be able to grasp the depth of the love I have for you. I am going to try my best to raise you to be a respectful, intelligent, kind, God-fearing man. I can only pray that the Lord above will guide me and give me the wisdom to do so.

Always know that Mommy loves you…no matter what.

Dear C. L. Thaines

I must say that I never would have guessed that you would do the things you have. A lot of women think about or even fantasize about sleeping with whom ever they please, but you take it to a whole other level. Some people might call you a slut or a whore and some women may even envy you, but all I can say is keep being you.

I remember the time you told me about sleeping with five guys in one weekend. I was blown away…maybe even a little disgusted but still curious. I listened to your sex tales and wondered how I would feel about myself if I did the same things. I mean, there have been guys that I've been attracted to, but I couldn't fathom sleeping with every guy I have ever been sexually attracted to.

If you were a guy, they would call you a pimp or player and give you all kinds of praise about how many people you've slept with, but because you're a woman, what you do is trashy, degrading and low class. How come it isn't all those things for a man? I some what envy you. I envy you solely because you have the courage to do what ever you want without thinking twice about what others will say or what they will think of you.

Now, don't get me wrong. I'm not saying I agree with all your escapades, but I do applaud your courage. Some times you just have to say, "screw them and what they think, this is my life". Keep doing your thing honey, just be careful. There are a lot of things out there now and some of them aren't curable.

Dear L. Wood,

*It's me again. I found a pile of my
early writings and I realized that you were the
inspiration for so many of them. They were all
about love, love lost and trying to rebuild. Reading
those poems brought me back to a time when my
emotions were raw, uncut, and unscripted. My
feelings were uncontrollable and overwhelming.
You were the first person to make me feel that way
and even with all the ups and downs, you still felt
so good to me.*

*At the time, I wanted our love to last a
lifetime and I honestly believed it could. The older
folks called it puppy love, but our puppy love felt
good. Despite our arguments, I still felt warm all
over when you spoke to me. I felt so appreciated
when you showed me you had been thinking of me*

Things I Should Have Said

and I felt so important and respected when you listened, really listened to me.

I don't know if you have a special some one in your life right now, but if you do I hope that she knows how wonderful of a person you are and pray that she treats you like a king. I hope that you find true happiness and success where ever you go. You were a beautiful person inside and out and I hope you always remain that way.

Best wishes.......

Dear Mom,

I wish that when I was growing up we had been closer. I wish that the first time I liked a boy I could have come to you and tell you. I wish so many things, but what is in the past is in the past and I know I shouldn't dwell on them, but I feel deep down in my heart, if I felt comfortable coming to you about things, I would be better off.

I am in no way trying to place blame on you for my emotional imbalance but I just wish we could have been friends back then. There were so many things I wanted to share with you, so many things I wanted learn from you, so many things I needed advice on. You did the best you could do given the circumstances and I am proud of your accomplishments. I know that underneath the strength you show is a woman with a tenderness and love unlike any other.

Things I Should Have Said

I know that you may not be fond of the way I go about getting things off my chest, but nevertheless you support me in all I do. I want to say thank you…again and again.

Dear Houston,

How are things? Is life finally coming together for you? I hope so. I heard you found yourself an apartment, got a new job and a new car...wow. I'm proud of you. You are making great changes in your life. Since I have to hear everything through the grape vine, I'm not always up to date with my information. It seems as if you have been eluding me. I've tried to email you and you didn't respond. What's the deal with that? I tried to call you just to find out the number has been disconnected. What is really going on?

When were younger we used to be close...closer than close. We had an unusual dynamic about our relationship. We weren't lovers, but more than friends. I'm going to be honest with you. Even when I had a boyfriend, I would still find

myself jealous of the time you spent with other
girls, yet when we were both single I was
completely content with knowing we were just
friends. Do you find that strange? I would even
find myself a little uneasy when another female
would ask me about you or flirt with you. I don't
know how to explain it, but that feeling has never
fully quite disappeared. I am involved in my own
relationship and I am content with it, but I miss
you. I want you to be happy with whom ever you
choose but I want you to be a part of my life.

We both know that when you went away, I
was there for you. I wrote to you all the time and
supported you. What happened to the loving
friendship we used to share? Has adulthood
compromised our ability to merely keep in touch?
Or is there something I don't know?

Well, I am not sure where you are in your
life and I am not sure what happened between us,

but I do know that I miss you very much and I would like to have you back in my life. I hope you are doing well.

Dear Carl P.,

So you think you love me? You haven't known me long enough to love me. You're more like infatuated with me and although I am very flattered, I cannot accept your proposal. You are very sweet and very caring, so I know that you will one day find the girl of your dreams, but unfortunately that girl isn't me.

When this all started we were just supposed to be friends. I think I might have been too nice to you and the occasional friendly flirting I did with you must have confused you. I am so sorry if you feel I have lead you on in anyway, but I must stop this before it gets out of hand. You told me last week that you can't wait to tell your mother about the big news. What big news? I hadn't accepted your marriage proposal. We had just decided that maybe we could be more than friends, not that we should be husband and wife. What am I missing? Where did we loose the connection? I am not ready to be married to any one, let alone to you.

I don't want to come off in a mean or negative way, but this definitely scares me. This came out of nowhere and I'm sorry to say that it will end up nowhere. Instead of working on a simple relationship, you have ruined what could have been by scaring me with marriage.

I don't know how else to say this but not only don't I think it is a good idea for us to get married, but I also don't think it would be wise if we continued a relationship. I am sorry if I hurt you in any way, but this is moving way too fast and before it spirals out of control, I must end it.

Dear J. Rich,

My mother was so happy when I started dating you. She was happy that I had found a nice, Christian boy to date. She thought you were something good to have happened to me; little did she know, your hormones were on over drive and you weren't the fun loving, innocent, church going boy she thought you were.

I met you at a church event and I too thought you were going to be different from the all the other guys who were just out to get in between someone's legs. I thought that because you seemed so into church that you wouldn't be so into sex, but boy was I wrong. There were so many conversations that always involved sex. I started to become annoyed with your sexual mentions and come-ons that it caused a problem in the relationship. We started to argue and fuss about things that were irrelevant. I remember my mother telling me I should try to work it out. I know she wanted me to work it out with you because you were a Christian, or so she thought. She wanted me to stick with a guy that she thought wouldn't pressure me for sex. She hadn't liked my previous boyfriend only because he wasn't of the same faith and she thought he was older than he said he was. In fact, that guy she didn't want me to be with was the one who was respectful, caring and unconcerned with sex. There was never any pressure with him, like there was with you.

Well, when we broke up I think my mother was displeased with my decision, but sometimes you just have to do things for yourself. I am glad I didn't stay with you. There was so much pressure from you, that if I had stayed and let you talk me *into something I was ready for, I would still be paying the cost today.*

I hope you have found some way to control your sexual urges or you have found the girl who will submit herself to them. Over all I hope you are happy and satisfied.

Dear Wayne,

I don't know what the hell is wrong with you. When we met you seemed normal and quite sane, but now you're acting crazy and deranged.

When this thing between us first started, you knew what the circumstances were. You knew what you were getting into. I still live at home and I still have rules to follow. I know you're a grown man, in college but you knew I was in the situation I was in. You were so cool and charming when we first met. You seemed to care about me and my feelings. You talked to me with respect and adoration. You made me feel secure, loved and cared for. You had such sincerity and genuine desire to be with me that I was blinded by it and didn't see the signs of what the future would hold.

I thought everything was good with you and going smoothly until you did something I never anticipated. I was in school that day and I had an argument with a guy I used to date. When I came home and we spoke on the phone you knew about what had happened and that scared me. You don't live anywhere near me, and you wouldn't have had any reason to be in the area. Were you spying in me or did you have one of your local friends do it? On another occasion I was waiting at the train station and had run into an old friend. Later that evening you interrogated me about who I was with all day and who I had been talking to. I should have known you were crazy from the first incidents but for some idiotic reason, I stayed around. Maybe I was fond of the idea that a guy in college would be interested in me, but now I see that all you want to do is control me. Telling me what I shouldn't wear, what I shouldn't eat and where I shouldn't go. Have you lost your mind?

I am writing you this letter to let you know that it is over. No need to call or write back. No need to discuss what you can do to make it better, we have already been there. Now it is just over. I can't take this crap any more and now I refuse to. So…goodbye.

Dear D. Field,

How come when we are on vacation we get along so well, but when we are at home there doesn't seem to be more between us than more than a couple of roommates? That is the question you asked me. You said you didn't want to go home and have to go back to us fighting with each other and being distant. So what's up? What's the deal with you? Why do I have to initiate affection? I feel like I have to beg you to hold my hand and why do I have to always ask you for a kiss?

You know, I love you very much and I would do anything for you but I sometimes I find myself thinking about other guys that I have been with who always made it known that they loved being with me, touching me and kissing me. I do things for you because I know that you like it. You don't think that you should have to do anything for me but provide for me financially. Well, unfortunately that isn't enough and there is going to come a time when I need someone to hold my hand and to give me sweet kisses. Will it be you or do I need to stop nagging you for affection and find it some where else? Damn, I don't want to cheat on you. I don't, I really don't. I want to be able to get everything I need from you. I need hugs and kisses. I want to be kissed goodnight, I want to be caressed gently and wrapped up in your arms.

I see other couples walking hand in hand and I'm jealous. I see them cuddling and stealing kisses and I want to cry. Some times I feel that you are so content with the fact that I'm already yours that you don't feel you have to or need to do those things anymore. How can I want to wear sexy lingerie to bed at night when I can't even get a few kisses through out the day? It's like you're pushing me away, telling me to go find what I want else where. It's so hard. I keep feeling rejected by you.

What am I to do? Would you prefer for me to go elsewhere? I know that can't be it. I become so fed up sometimes; I want to go searching for someone to hold me. You don't show me very much attention anymore. I need some attention from you and if I can't get it, I will be forced to get it from someone else. I can't live without hugs and kisses. I need them in my life in order to be happy. I am already feeling guilty and I haven't even ventured outside of you yet. And it pains me to use the word 'yet' but the truth is that if I don't get it from you, it is inevitable that I will get from some one else. Don't make me find what I need from someone else. Don't make me cheat; don't make me break up with you. Please, don't make me do this. Please, consider what I have said. I desperately need some affection and attention from you.

Things I Should Have Said

Dear G. R. Lore,

We definitely have an odd friendship. I can't even recall how we became the way we are. We don't speak very often, better yet we only speak on occasion but I know that when ever I call you I can count you. If I ever have a problem, I know you will be there for me any way you can.

It feels contradictory to say that you are the closest friend I have yet, we rarely hang out and we rarely speak. How can I say you are my closest friend? Yet, how can I not. I hope you know that when ever you need me I am here not only to listen, but to help. You have a good heart and I am blessed to have a friend like you. A friend that I can call on no matter what.

I want you to know that I as rare as our encounters and conversations are, I appreciate every one of them. I know this letter is short, but hopefully I made my point clear. Just want to say

thanks for being my friend. I love you for that and I

am proud to have a friend like you.

Dear Mr. L. Wood

You are definitely 'going through some things' as you put it. I just want you to know that you have once again offended me and this time, I don't feel the need to 'fix' the issue. What you are dealing with is probably far more than I am imagining, but not beyond my intellectual capacity.

I too, am dealing with some very complex issues in this stage of my life and I for some idiotic reason, thought that maybe you and I could be friends. Friends who were there to just be an open ear. We have history together and a history that wasn't all that bad. We had fun when we were together and if I do recall correctly we enjoyed one another's conversations, right?

What I also remember is that you had a difficult time expression yourself and I see that even after 5 years and life experiences, you still have difficulty doing so. It is unfortunate that you feel you cannot trust me, but the up side of that is not only have I never given you a reason not to trust me in the past, but I am not asking for your trust now.

I will not avoid discussing what we did, but I clearly expressed to you that I am not looking for an emotional connection, nor am I looking for a relationship. I am not ready, willing or able to give my heart, mind and soul to anyone. On top of my own personal reasons, you too are emotionally beaten down and unwilling and unready to give yourself to anyone in that way.

What I offered was simple and honest. I wanted to be your friend and have you as a friend in return. I am not looking to build a relationship with you or reignite any old flames. Just someone to talk to and hang out with occasionally.

I naively thought that maybe it would help if we both had someone to talk to who wasn't as directly involved and a part of what we were already dealing with in both of our lives. You know, like somewhat of an escape from our currently troubles… but silly me.

As I told you once before, a long time ago…I will be your friend until you tell me not to. I still, have always and will always care about you deeply. I hope that whatever it is that you are going through works itself out and you become a better man because of it. You know how to reach me.

Dear KV.

I know it's been a long time and I know that I haven't been a very good friend over the past few years and well basically, I want to apologize. I want to apologize for the way I 'broke off' our friendship. I should not have gone about it that way. At the time, I will admit that I felt a little overwhelmed by you. I felt almost as if you and I were dating and I had to make time for you in that sense.

I ran into your sister the other day and boy have times changed. In earlier years she would have been excited to see me and embrace me uncontrollably, but instead she just made a comment to the effect of "I didn't know you were going to be in town" and walked away. She did not embrace me in the manner in which I had become accustomed, nor did she utter another word to me. If I recall correctly, she avoided looking in my direction thereafter.

I am not sure that had I gotten a warmer welcome if I would have even been inclined to receive it with a positive attitude. The feelings that I have for the people back home have changed dramatically. I still and will always love and care for them, but the reality of it is that we're are on different paths in life…and these paths do not seem to be running parallel nor do they seem as if they will someday cross again.

I am writing to you in hopes that you are doing well and have forgiven me for my failure at being your friend. I am not assuming that you will again embrace me as the best friend I once was to you but more so, I'm asking for forgiveness. If it is in your heart to reach out to me upon reading this, please do so because I would be more than happy to hear from you and have you back in my life.

Once again, I want to say that I am truly sorry for failing you and I hope that this finds you in good health and happiness. I will always love and care for you, no matter how far apart we grow. Always, always remember that.

Dear Ex of my Ex,

I gave all of myself to you…mind, body and soul. And look what you have done to me. I thought that you were someone I could spend a lifetime with, but apparently I over estimated. You are a liar and a cheater. I trusted you with my thoughts, my emotions and my body yet you betrayed each one.

How can you now look me in the eye and act as if what you did was just a simple and silly little mistake? You are right; people do make mistakes once maybe even twice, but not over and over again. Then you continue to lie to me which clearly indicates that you do not love or respect me. You are not even worth the words I now write on this page, but I need to let my thoughts and feelings run free.

I want you to know just how much I loved you and would have done anything for you but you played me for a fool and a fool I was if you were able to do the things you did right under my nose. Maybe I was in denial, maybe I was naïve, or maybe I was just too in love to see the truth. They say love is blind and utterly blind I was. I had decided to just let go of any inhibitions, any fear I had had and just let us be.

Now what a mess you have created. I won't say 'never', but it will take me a very long time and/or a very special person to give me that optimistic view I once had of people and relationships. You have made it unfairly that much more difficult for the next individual who may come along. I am not going to sit here and be 'the bigger person' and say things that at the moment aren't true, like; "I wish you well, hope you find someone who makes you happy". I would be lying through

Things I Should Have Said   95

my teeth if I did because to be quite honest, I want you to feel what you made me feel. Pain. Despair. Betrayal. Sorrow.

My eyes are now open to who you truly are and I will never play that kind of fool again. Thanks to you, everyone is guilty until proven innocent.

-From his perspective

Dear Mary Beth,

So, I hear from a mutual friend that you have made some negative comments about me. I have thought for a long time now that I should expect that from you, but I guess the affirmation just makes it a little clearer now just how far apart we have grown.

I am also aware that you have found my replacement. Wow! I guess I was dispensable after all. And all along I thought I was a friend you thought highly of and who might have even held a little value. I guess I was wrong. I'm sure the substitute Me is doing a fine job, and if you have upgraded to an even better friend, then by all means, be happy and forget me. I hope the replacement does exactly as you need, want and expect.

We've have known each other for quite some time now and though we have gradually grown distant over the past few years, I still care about you and wish you well. We may never be as close as we once were and I don't even expect or hope for that, but somewhere deep inside me would like to have you as a friend again.

I am not ignorant to the fact that your 'circle of friends' no longer include me, but I can admit that I am saddened that a decade old friendship could be so easily lost. In any event, I hope that you are happy now and just so you know, I forgive you for what happened to me that night.

Dear Ike C. Steven,

I thought about you the other day. What has become of you? Are you well? Are you still married? I remember your flirtatious smile and subtle conversation and how you always did have an appeal about you.

Are the young women falling prey to your predatory glances? (Smile) I know that as one gets older, it is uplifting to know that younger individuals of the opposite sex still find you attractive.

To be honest with you though, I am not sure what to believe about you. Are you just the habitual flirt or are you really a cheater? Had I succumb to your intriguing smile and captivating conversations, would I have been a victim of your sexual rendezvous'? Now that I look back on things,

I have to wonder if you were just looking for someone to stroke your ego or if you were really on the prowl. Was I just another girl or was there ever any genuine interest?

In my mind and from what you had shown me during the brief time I knew you, you seemed sincere in your words and actions. Though, I do feel that the flirting you did with me was more than your wife would tolerate, I think she would at least be pleased that you didn't take it to a physical level... at least not with me. Who is to say you didn't get physical with other young women.

Anyway, I hope life is treating you well, you're still being a good father to those boys of yours, and that whether still married or divorced; you are happy.

Dear Nicole R.

I know that I don't know you very well, and you may feel it isn't my place to say what I am about to say, but I feel I have played my position and held my tongue long enough. I must express my opinions, which I am entitled to.

I can't understand how love has blinded you so much so that you disrespect your own mother. It is was one thing, when you didn't spend time with people with whom you were once very close to and you carry yourself differently (not in a good way), but it is another to 'bite the hand that feeds you'.

Has your self respect been lowered along with your self esteem or do you just not give a damn? You have been burning bridges on account of decisions you have made over the past two years or so and I am weary of what may become of you when the walls around you come tumbling down.

Who will you turn to when the people who were once there for you can no longer bare the burden of helping you? Isn't it unfortunate that simply being there for you is now a burden in the eyes of your family and friends? This isn't something to be proud of, nor is it something you should let go unattended.

Your family will always love you no matter what, but that doesn't obligate them to be supportive of your bad decisions or condone your disrespectful words and behavior. I hope that one day; someone will say something or do something to open your eyes. I hope that what ever it is you're seeking; you find. I pray that the hearts of those around you will not be utterly hardened if and when your finally decide to turn a new leaf.

Dear DJ,

I just want to say that even though we rarely see one another lately, I truly do care about you and have genuine concern for you. To get straight to the point, I want to tell you how I feel about your current boyfriend.

I know you love him, or least you think you do and love is a wonderful thing, if it is real. I am not saying that your love for him is not real, because I am positive it is.

I don't know how you behaved in your relationship before the incident occurred but I do know if he could lie to you about sleeping with someone, he could lie to you about much more. Have you taken the time to consider that if he wasn't straight forward about sleeping with someone else, he may be hiding other things surrounding the situation? What if he didn't wear protection? What if he had gotten her pregnant? What would you have done then? Can you imagine if the shoe was on the other foot; what he would have done? Do you honestly think that he would have taken you back had you slept with someone else and then lied about it? Think really hard on this one; he's a man and they say that men have a harder time forgiving a woman for sleeping with someone else, than the other way around.

I know it sounds like I am being very negative regarding your relationship and possibly your happiness, but I don't feel he deserves someone like you. You have a lot going for you and he doesn't appreciate you for all that you are. You are intelligent, kind, caring and genuine.

I just want you to know and believe that you are worth much more than he can offer or is willing to offer you.

… Then again, I could be wrong about him. Maybe he is truly is remorseful and will never ever do that to you again. Maybe he has learned his lesson and will be truthful from here on out. Then again…

Dear Jo-Jo,

I saw you the other night at a club while I was out with a new guy I am currently dating. You came up to me and said I looked familiar, and then you asked me where you might have seen me before. I was shocked and speechless. The only thing I could think was, 'You have got to be kidding me. This is not happening.' I told you a fake name and said that it was impossible for you to have known me and walked back to my date shivering.

He said I looked like I had just seen a ghost and asked if I was alright. I still could barely speak, so I just shook my head and sat down. My date was very concerned and feared that someone had harassed me on my way to or from the restroom, but I was finally able to reassure him that I was fine.

I spotted you across the room and kept a watchful eye on you for the remainder of the night. All the feelings that I thought I had finally gotten over came rushing back with a force that I almost couldn't contain.

I remembered how you had dragged me to your room and threw me on the bed. I remembered how heavy my limbs felt and how I wish my friend would come rescue me. I remembered how I had cried that night when I finally got home. I remembered how my blood was on your shirt and how your friends had surprised, almost shocked looks on their faces.

It had been years…seven to be exact and I thought I had finally moved on with my life. I knew I would never emotionally be the same but I thought I had found a way to cope with my past, but I was wrong. I will never ever really be over the pain you put me through, but I pray that one day I will be able to have and maintain a healthy relationship with someone who loves and understands me.

Dear Friends and Family,

I hope the letters is this book do not offend but inspire you to never have unfinished business. I hope that it helps you to be better able to confess your true feelings no matter how unwelcome, surprising, or disappointing they may be. I thank you all for your inspiration. To those of you with whom I've lost touch, please know and believe that I will never forget you. To those of you who are still apart of my life, I would like to take this opportunity to say that I love having you in my life and hope that I fulfill your expectations. I hope you know that I am a better person because of my trials and my errors. I cannot to be a perfect person, but I can promise that if you need me, I will always try for you. I am no longer as selfish as I once was and I will be there when you need me. I will not guarantee that you will always like what I have to say, but I can guarantee that I will be honest.

Dear God,

It's me again. As I write these words, I find myself torn between two decisions; following my dreams or taking the more realistic approach. I don't want to keep pushing my dreams aside and miss out on the opportunity to fulfill my dreams and achieve my goals, but I have to be responsible.

How do I decide what is right and what is wrong? Aren't I supposed to know just know when something good is knocking at my door? I feel like I would be a fool not to take the chance and live my dreams, then again I feel like it would be foolish to jeopardize all that I know and love.

I want to ask that you show me the way to through the right door and help me to follow through with anything I start. I want to thank you for your love and kindness. I want to thank you for the many opportunities you have already afforded me and for the opportunities that have yet to be shown to me.

I pray that you continue to bless my family and I in all aspects of our lives and teach each of us how to be humble and kind. I pray you forgive us of who we are and be gracious unto us.

Dear Reader,

Thank you for choosing this book today. I hope that it was inspirational and eye opening. I hope that you continue to support me in my literary endeavors. Please look out for my next book, Forbidden Fruit.

-Simone

www.ingramcontent.com/pod-product-compliance
Lightning Source LLC
Chambersburg PA
CBHW031845170626
46807CB00004B/1625